A Beginning-to-Read Book

It's Bedtime, Dear Dragon

by Margaret Hillert

Illustrated by David Schimmell

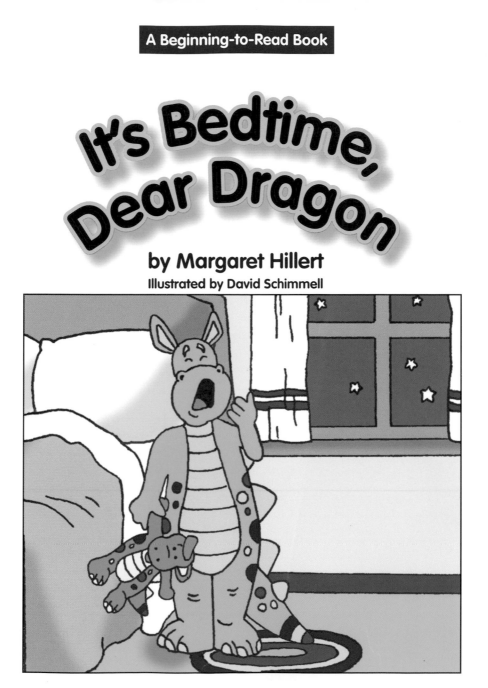

NORWOOD HOUSE PRESS

DEAR CAREGIVER, The *Beginning-to-Read* series is a carefully written collection of classic readers you may remember from your own childhood. Each book features text comprised of common sight words to provide your child ample practice reading the words that appear most frequently in written text. The many additional details in the pictures enhance the story and offer the opportunity for you to help your child expand oral language and develop comprehension.

Begin by reading the story to your child, followed by letting him or her read familiar words and soon your child will be able to read the story independently. At each step of the way, be sure to praise your reader's efforts to build his or her confidence as an independent reader. Discuss the pictures and encourage your child to make connections between the story and his or her own life. At the end of the story, you will find reading activities and a word list that will help your child practice and strengthen beginning reading skills.

Above all, the most important part of the reading experience is to have fun and enjoy it!

Shannon Cannon

Shannon Cannon,
Literacy Consultant

Norwood House Press • P.O. Box 316598 • Chicago, Illinois 60631
For more information about Norwood House Press please visit our website at *www.norwoodhousepress.com* or call 866-565-2900.

Text copyright ©2012 by Margaret Hillert. Illustrations and cover design copyright ©2012 by Norwood House Press, Inc. All rights reserved. No part of this book may be reproduced or utilized in any form or by any means without written permission from the publisher.

LIBRARY OF CONGRESS CATALOGING-IN-PUBLICATION DATA
    Hillert, Margaret.
     It's bedtime dear dragon / by Margaret Hillert ; illustrated by David Schimmell.
       p. cm. -- (A beginning-to-read book)
     Summary: "After dinner a boy and his pet dragon do schoolwork, take out
the recycling and prepare for bedtime, by taking a bath and putting away
toys"--Provided by publisher.
     ISBN-13: 978-1-59953-503-6 (library edition : alk. paper)
     ISBN-10: 1-59953-503-3 (library edition : alk. paper)
     ISBN-13: 978-1-60357-383-2 (e-book)
     ISBN-10: 1-60357-383-6 (e-book)
    [1. Bedtime--Fiction. 2. Dragons--Fiction.] I. Schimmell, David, ill. II.
Title. III. Title: It is bedtime dear dragon. PZ7.H558Iq 2012
    [E]--dc23
                2011038943
Manufactured in the United States of America in North Mankato, Minnesota
              203R—052012

I can do this work.
I like to help you Mother.

I like it, too.
Can you help me with this?
Take this out, and then
do your schoolwork.

4

Yes I can do that.

This bag goes in the green box.

And I will do my schoolwork now.

Did you do your schoolwork?

Yes, Mother.
See? I did it all.
It is good work.

Here are some little cookies to eat,
You will like this!

Yes, Mother I like little cookies!

Now I want to go to bed.
But I have to do some more things.

I will put all my toys away.
I can do this.
The toys go into this big box.

Now we have to do this.
It is good to do this.

And I have to do this.
You cannot do it.

Father. Can you come and read a fun book now? I want you.

Here I am.

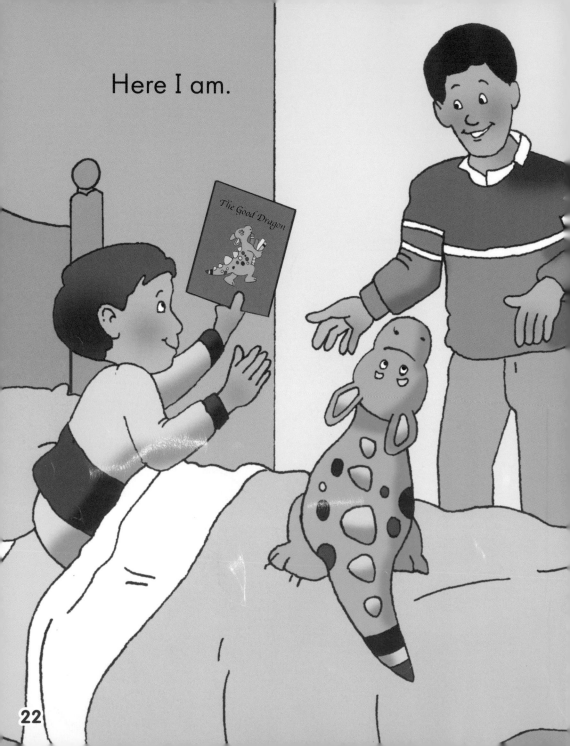

This is a book with
a dragon in it.
He is a good dragon.

See what he can do.

And he can do this——

And this!

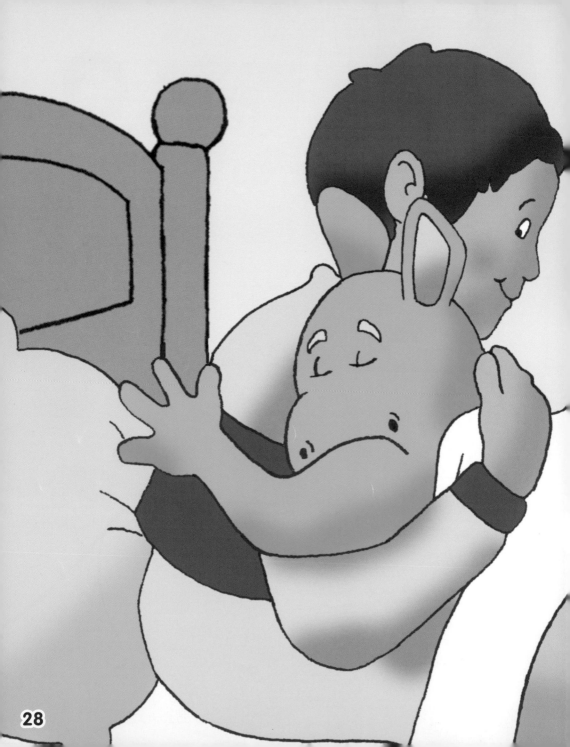

You are a good dragon too.
I love you, Dear Dragon.

The following activities support the findings of the National Reading Panel that determined the most effective components for reading instruction are: Phonemic Awareness, Phonics, Vocabulary, Fluency, and Text Comprehension.

Phonemic Awareness: The /b/ sound

Sound Substitution: Say the words on the left to your child. Ask your child to repeat the word, changing the first sound to /**b**/:

kite = bite	felt = belt	pat = bat	fun = bun
corn = born	fox = box	leak = beak	path = bath
goat = boat	turn = burn	mall = ball	glue = blue

Phonics: The Letter Bb

1. Demonstrate how to form the letters **B** and **b** for your child.

2. Have your child practice writing **B** and **b** at least three times each.

3. Ask your child to point to the words in the book that start with the letter **b**.

4. Write down the following words and ask your child to circle the letter **b** in each word:

bat	cab	barn	rub	cub
bird	bib	bed	baby	book
marble	bit	tub	crib	maybe

Vocabulary: Compound Words

1. Explain to your child that sometimes two words can be put together to make a new word. These are called compound words. The story has three compound words: bedtime, cannot and schoolwork.

2. Write down the following words on separate pieces of paper:

news	plane	board	base	bed	fly
box	butter	week	ball	paper	room
sand	air	house	skate	dog	end

3. Help your child move the pieces of paper around to form compound words. *Possible answers: newspaper, airplane, skateboard, baseball, bedroom, butterfly, sandbox, weekend, doghouse*

Fluency: Shared Reading

1. Reread the story to your child at least two more times while your child tracks the print by running a finger under the words as they are read. Ask your child to read the words he or she knows with you.

2. Reread the story taking turns, alternating readers between sentences or pages.

Text Comprehension: Discussion Time

1. Ask your child to retell the sequence of events in the story.

2. To check comprehension, ask your child the following questions:

   · What are some of the things the boy does before going to bed?

   · Why does the boy put the bag in the green box?

   · What is the green box for?

   · Why do you think the dragon cannot brush his teeth?

   · What are some things that you do before you go to bed at night?

WORD LIST

***It's Bedtime, Dear Dragon* uses the 68 words listed below.**
This list can be used to practice reading the words that appear in the text.
You may wish to write the words on index cards and use them to help your
child build automatic word recognition. Regular practice with these words
will enhance your child's fluency in reading connected text.

a	dear	I	put	we
all	did	in		what
am	do	into	read	will
and	dragon	is		with
are		it	schoolwork	work
away	eat		see	
		like	some	yes
bag	Father	little		you
bed	fun	love	take	your
big			that	
book	go	me	the	
box	goes	more	then	
but	good	Mother	things	
	green	my	this	
can			to	
cannot	have	now	too	
come	he		toys	
cookies	help	out		
	here		want	

ABOUT THE AUTHOR Margaret Hillert has written over 80 books for
children who are just learning to read. Her books
have been translated into many different languages and over a million children
throughout the world have read her books. She first started writing poetry as
a child and has continued to write for children and adults throughout her life. A
first grade teacher for 34 years, Margaret is now retired from teaching and lives in
Michigan where she likes to write, take walks in the morning, and care for her three cats.

Photograph by Glenna Washburn

ABOUT THE ADVISER Shannon Cannon contributed the activities pages that appear in
this book. Shannon serves as a literacy consultant and provides
staff development to help improve reading instruction. She is a frequent presenter at educational
conferences and workshops. Prior to this she worked as an elementary school teacher and as
president of a curriculum publishing company.